KT-527-203

Every new generation of children is enthralled by the famous stories in our Well-loved Tales series. Younger ones love to have the story read to them. Older children will enjoy the exciting stories in an easy-to-read text.

Published by Ladybird Books Ltd Loughborough Leicestershire UK
Ladybird Books Inc Lewiston Maine 04240 USA

The Emperor's New Clothes

retold for easy reading
by LYNNE BRADBURY

illustrated by SALLY LONG

The author's fee was donated to the International Year of the Child Fund

Ladybird Books

Long ago, there lived an Emperor who *loved* new clothes. He had clothes for the morning. He had different clothes for the afternoon. And he had special clothes for the evening.

One day two wicked men came to the town.

"We make cloth," said one man.

"Yes, we are weavers," said the other man.

"We can make very special cloth,"

said both men together.

The Emperor was very pleased. He
wanted some new cloth to make a
special new suit
of clothes.

"Tell me about your special cloth,"
said the Emperor.

The weavers told the Emperor that their cloth was so special that anyone who couldn't see it must be very stupid. The Emperor was even more pleased.

The weavers wanted to start work.

"We need gold thread," they said.

The Emperor gave them lots and

lots of gold thread to make their

special cloth.

But the wicked weavers stole the
gold thread. They hid it in their
bags.

Then they pretended to make the special cloth. The weavers worked very hard. The loom which makes cloth went backwards and forwards. Click, clack, click, clack, it went.

13

One night the Emperor wanted to
know if the gold cloth was ready.
He sent his Prime Minister to have
a look.

"Come and tell me if the cloth is beautiful," ordered the Emperor.

The Prime Minister went to see the
weavers. They were working very
hard. Click, clack, click, clack,
went the loom. The Prime Minister
looked and looked.

"Oh dear!" he thought. "I can't
see anything. But *I* am not
stupid." So he said to the weavers,
"It's beautiful cloth. I'll tell the
Emperor."

When he had gone, the weavers
laughed and laughed. Then they
said, "We need some more gold
thread to make this special cloth."

The Emperor let them have lots
more gold thread. The wicked
weavers stole the thread and hid it
in their bags.

Then they worked harder than ever.
Click, clack, click, clack, click,
went the loom.

The Prime Minister told the
Emperor that the cloth was very
beautiful. Soon, everyone was
talking about the Emperor's new
suit.

The next night, the Emperor
wanted someone else to look at the
cloth for his new suit. This time he
sent the Captain of the Guard.

"Come and tell me if it is
finished," ordered the Emperor.

The Captain went to see the
weavers. They were still working
very hard. Click, clack, click,

clack, click, went the loom.

The Captain looked and looked. "Oh dear!" he thought. "I can't see anything. But the Prime Minister could see the cloth and *I* am not stupid."

The Captain told the weavers, "It's beautiful cloth. The Emperor will be pleased. I'll tell him."

25

When he had gone, the weavers
laughed and laughed. Then they
worked faster and faster.

Soon the weavers said that the

special cloth was made. Now they
pretended to cut the cloth into
pieces. They began to sew the
pieces together to make the
Emperor's new suit of clothes.

The next day the weavers said,
"Please can the Emperor come and
try on his new suit? Then we can
finish the sewing." The Emperor
was very pleased. He went to see
the weavers.

"Oh dear! I can't see the cloth!"
said the Emperor, to himself. "The
Prime Minister and the Captain of
the Guard could see it. *I* am not
stupid." So the Emperor said,
"This is beautiful cloth. These will
be my very best clothes."

Now it was time to try on his suit.
The weavers made the Emperor
take off his clothes. Then he had
to stand still. The weavers made
sure that the new suit would fit the
Emperor.

He felt cold but he said, "This will be a beautiful suit of clothes. The cloth is so light that I can hardly feel it."

When the Emperor had gone, the weavers laughed and laughed. They said they must sew faster and faster so that the new clothes would be finished.

Everyone in the land had heard about the new suit. In two days there was going to be a parade in the town. The Emperor was going to wear his new clothes in the parade. Everyone would be there to see him.

At the end of the
next day, the weavers said that the
new suit of clothes was finished.
Everyone went to look.

The Prime Minister said, "It's a
wonderful new suit."

And the Captain of the Guard
said, "I have never seen such
beautiful clothes."

Then came the day of the parade.
The weavers helped the Emperor to
dress. They made sure his suit was
just right and then they put his
crown on his head.

"Your majesty, you look
wonderful!" said the weavers. And
the Emperor gave the weavers two
big bags of gold.

The Emperor was very, very pleased with his new clothes.

"All the people will look at me," he said to himself. He went out to join the parade.

The people of the town had hung flags from their houses. They stood at the sides of the roads waiting for the Emperor to pass by.

Then the parade started and all the people began to shout and wave.

Everyone had heard about the special cloth. They had been told that only stupid people could not see it.

"The Emperor's new clothes are beautiful," said one man.

"Doesn't he look wonderful!" said an old woman.

"This is a very special suit," said another man.

"Yes! Yes!" shouted all the people.

The Emperor was very happy.
"These are the best clothes I've
ever had," he said. He laughed
and waved to all the people and
they waved back at him.

The parade was nearly finished. The Emperor thought that it had been the best day in his life.

Then suddenly, a little boy pointed at the Emperor. The boy began to laugh. "The Emperor has nothing on!" he shouted.

And all the people began to laugh too.

The Emperor knew that he had been tricked. "I *am* very stupid," he thought. His face went very, very red.

Of course, the weavers had gone!